AF086381

Tell the Robots

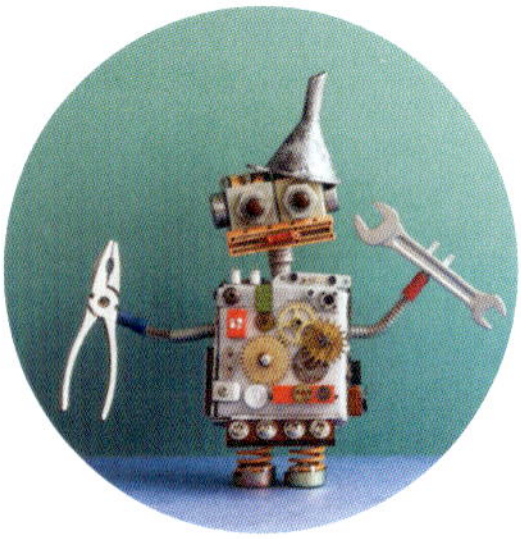

Written by
Stephen Rickard

Ransom

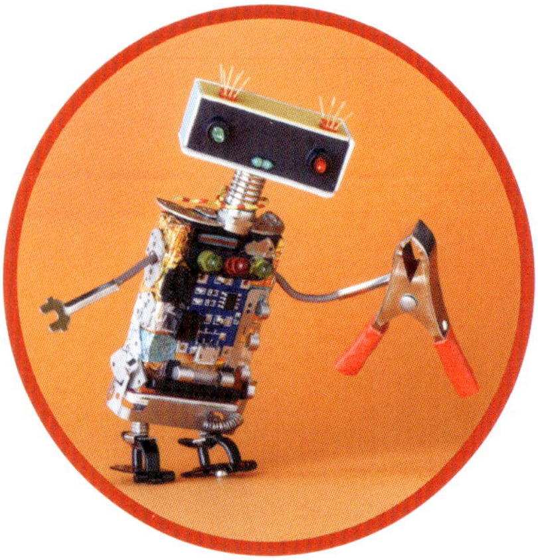
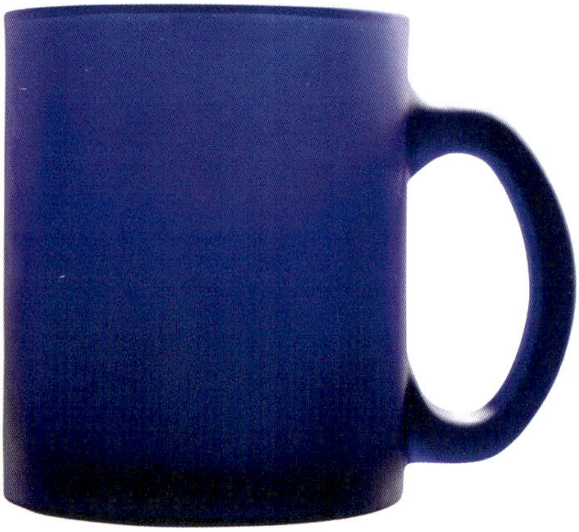
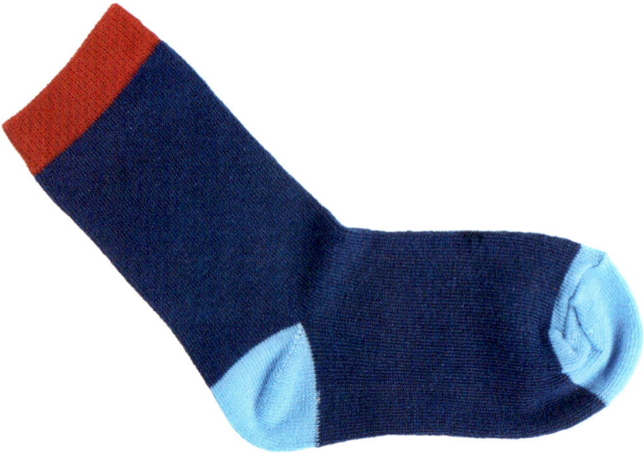
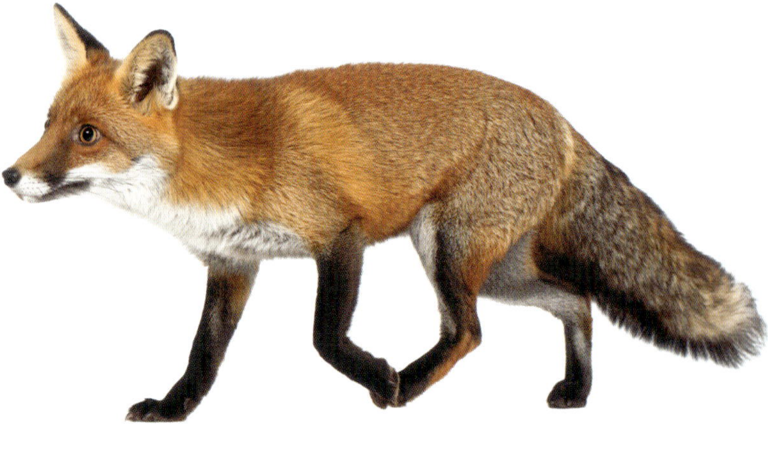

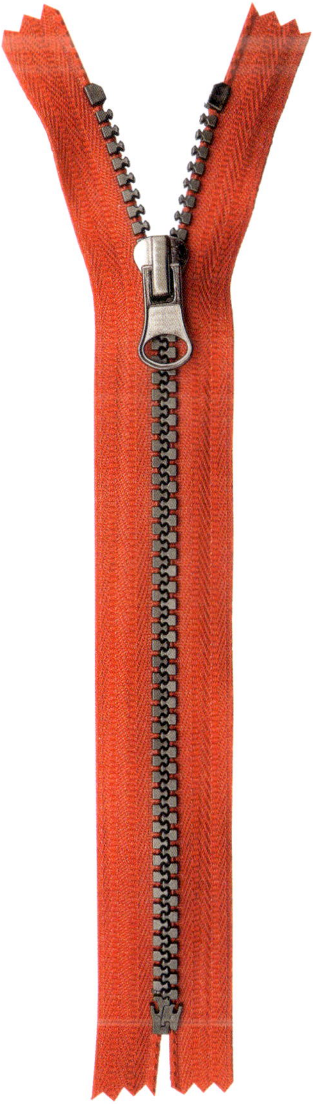

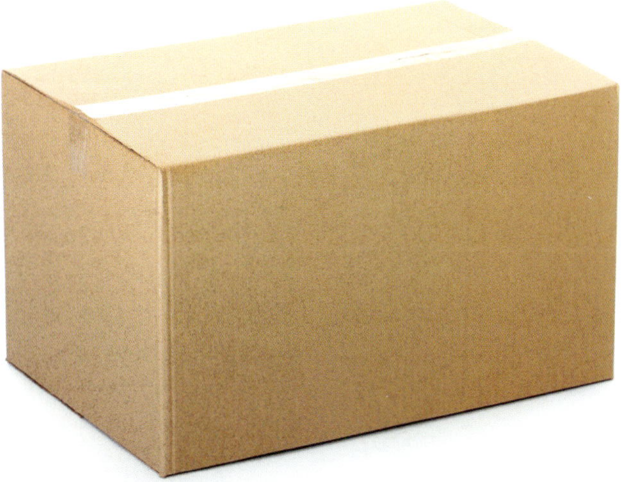

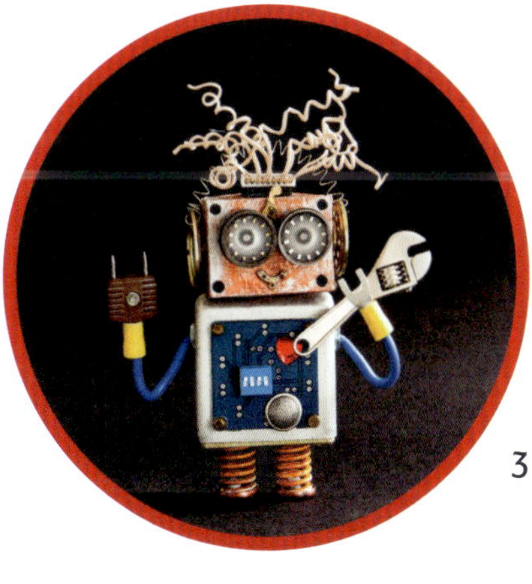

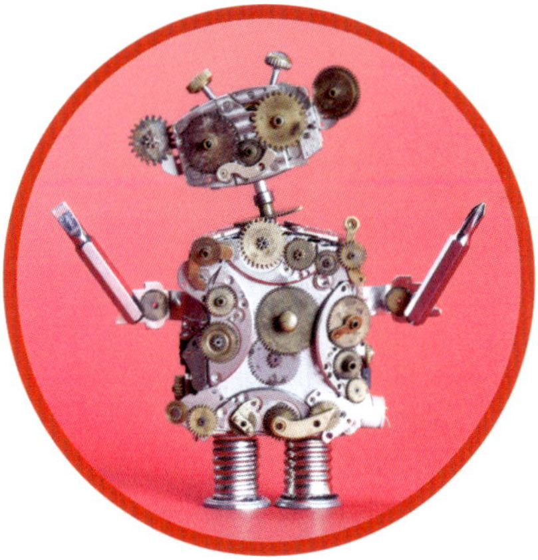

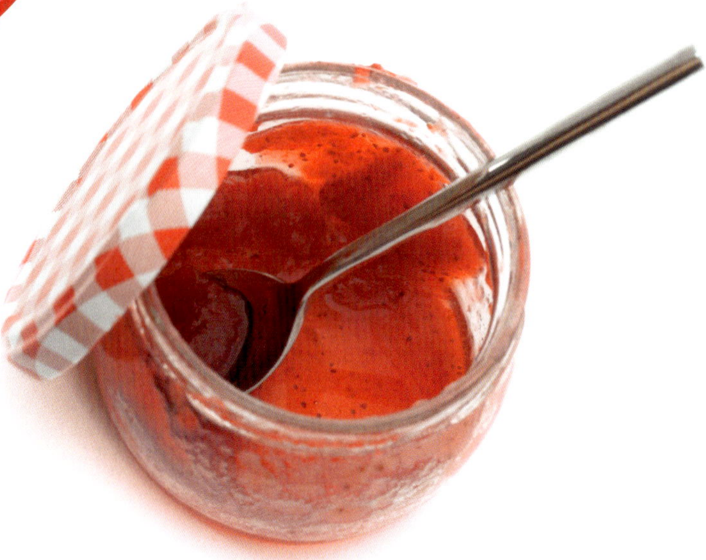

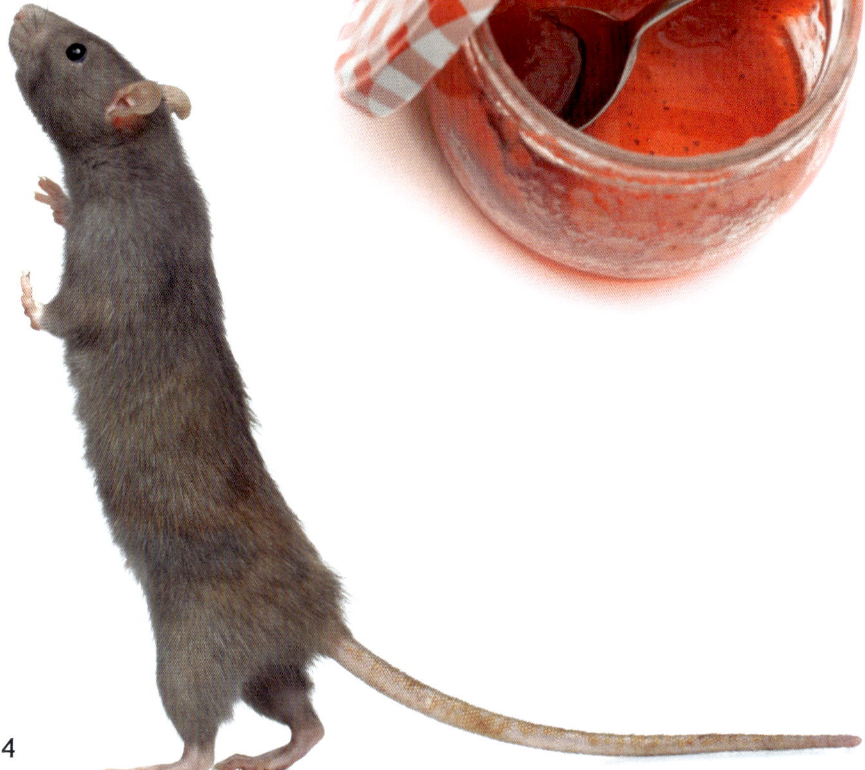

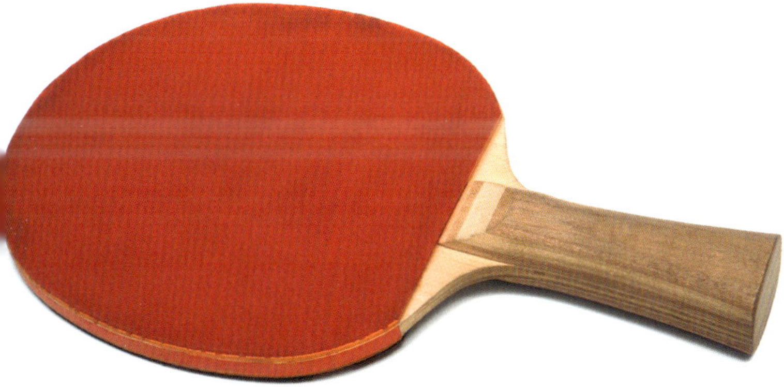

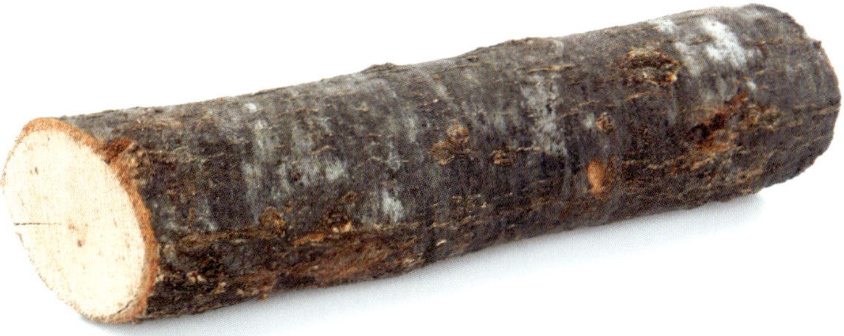

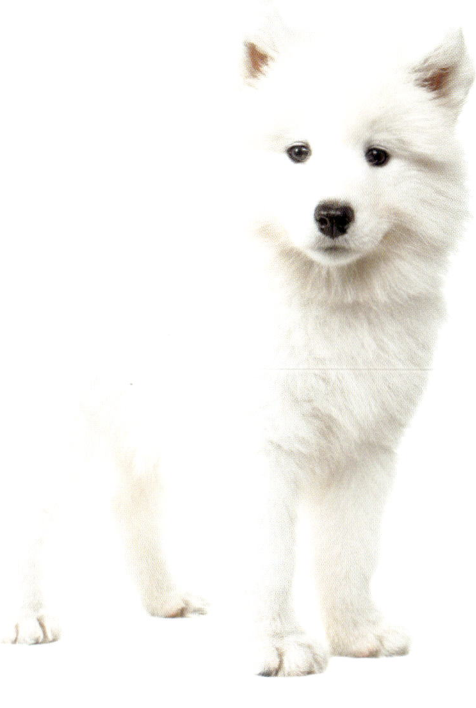

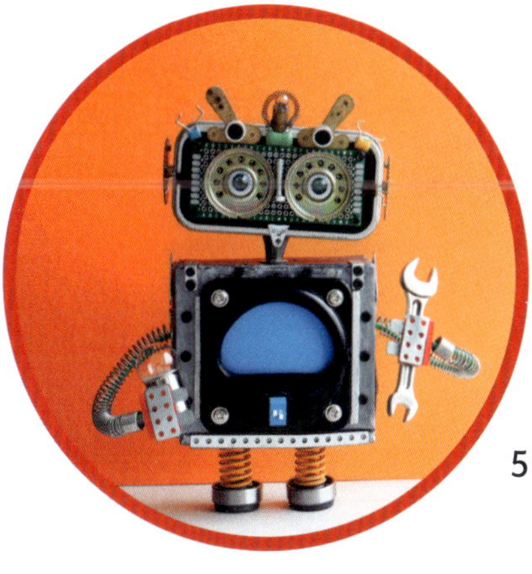

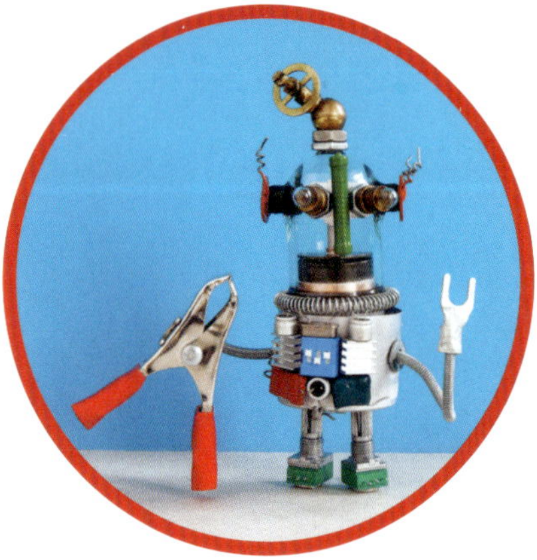

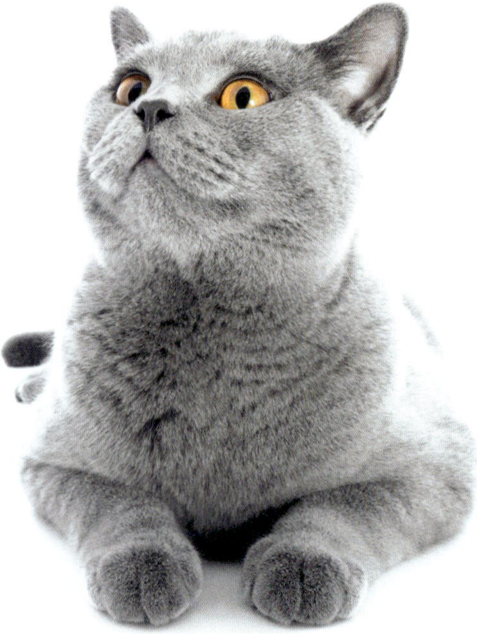

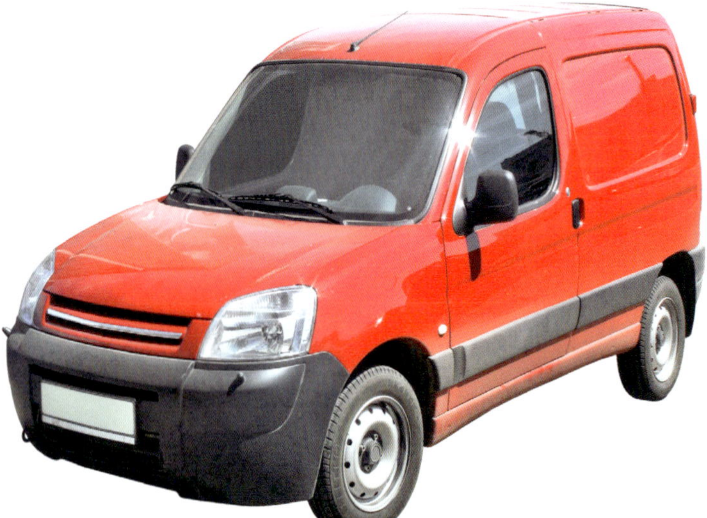

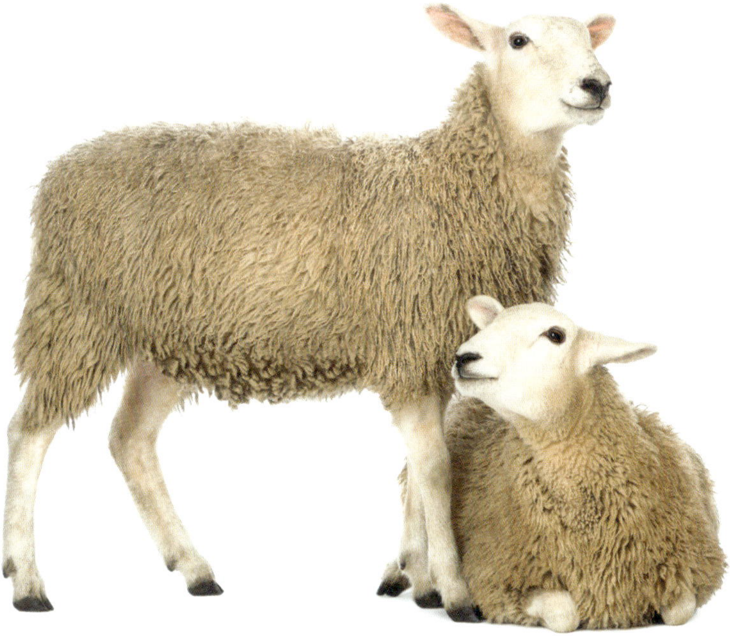

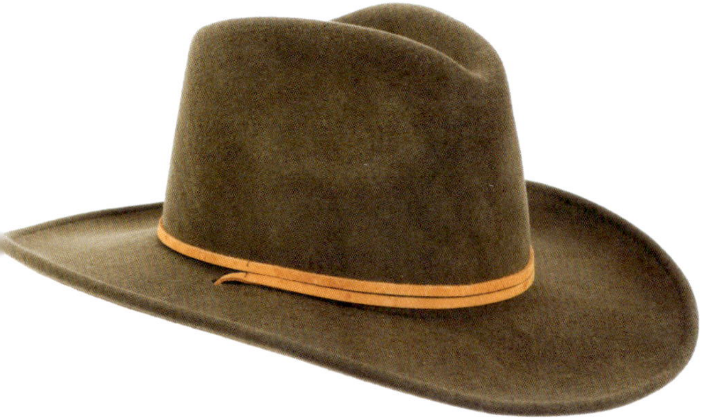

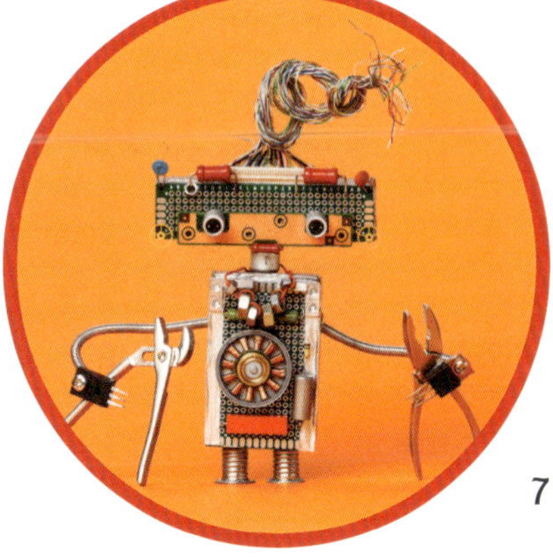

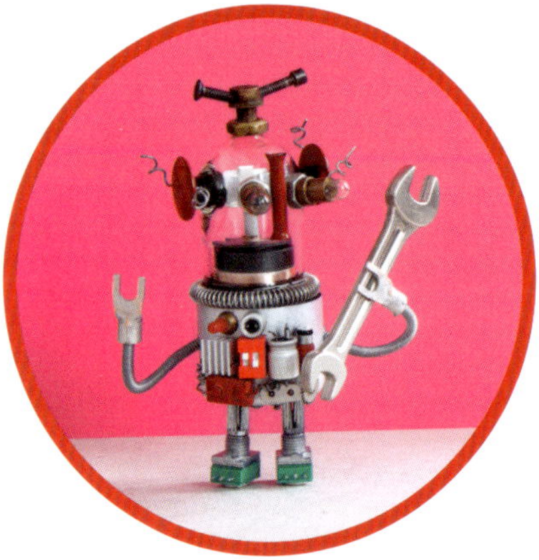

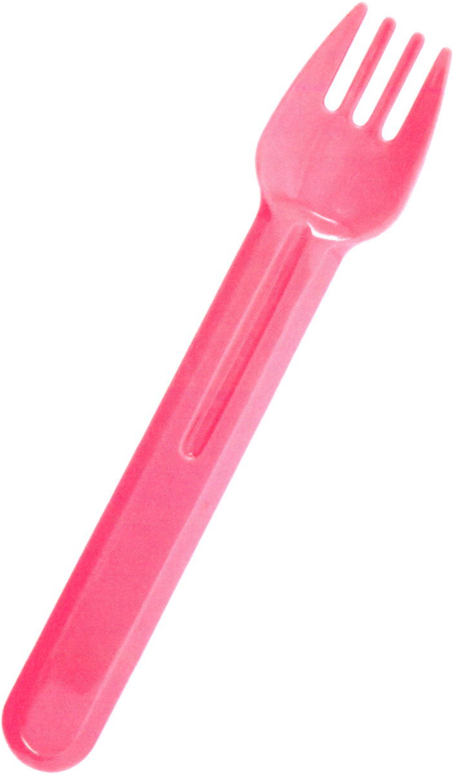

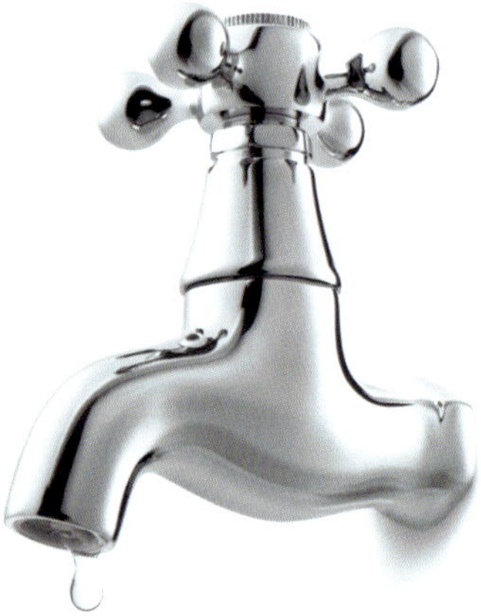

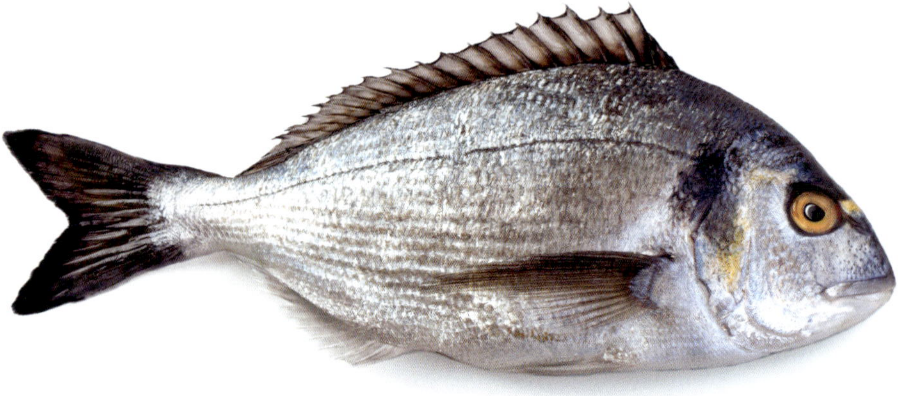